UNICORN'S SECRET

#2

The Silver Thread

by Kathleen Duey
illustrated by Omar Rayyan

ALADDIN PAPERBACKS

New York   London   Toronto   Sydney   Singapore

First Aladdin Paperbacks edition December 2001
Text copyright © 2001 by Kathleen Duey
Illustrations copyright © 2001 by Omar Rayyan

Aladdin Paperbacks
An imprint of Simon & Schuster
Children's Publishing Division
1230 Avenue of the Americas
New York, NY 10020

Designed by Debra Sfetsios
The text of this book was set in Golden Cockerel ITC.
Printed in the United States of America
2 4 6 8 10 9 7 5 3

ISBN 0-689-84270-8
Library of Congress Control Number 2001095837

✦

Heart can't remember her parents. She can't remember anything before the day Simon Pratt found her sleeping in the river grass near Ash Grove. He took her in. But the villagers wouldn't trust a girl without memories. Heart's only friend in Ash Grove was Ruth Oakes, the healer. Now, Heart is wandering in Lord Dunraven's endless forests, alone.

Well . . . not exactly *alone*.

✦

✦ CHAPTER ONE

Heart shivered on a high ridge.

The sun was rising over Lord Dunraven's vast forest.

She couldn't see the village of Ash Grove or the Blue River.

But she knew where they were—a long day's walk, straight east on the Derrytown road.

Heart stretched, shaking off her dream.

Every night in the woods, she'd had the same one.

In it, she was always running; something was chasing her.

She woke every morning to the sound of forest birds singing.

Her pulse would slow and her fear would fade.

Heart sighed, looking down the slope. The trees spread out in every direction. Lord Dunraven's forests really were *endless.*

Heart wondered, as she did every morning, if Tin Blackaby's men were searching for her. They had seen her running away from Ash Grove.

But how important was a ragged girl with a scarred mare and a spindly colt?

Would they care where she went?

Heart had stayed away from the Derrytown road.

Both Avamir and Moonsilver were white, after all.

Any sharp-eyed traveler might spot them.

Heart glanced at them. From a distance, they *did* look like any mare and colt.

They weren't, of course.

As strange as it still seemed to Heart, they were unicorns.

Unicorns!

Heart smiled.

No one back in Ash Grove believed in unicorns

even though everyone knew the legend about the town's name.

It was an odd story. Storytellers said a unicorn had touched the Blue River with her horn. The water had exploded into steam so hot that the grove of ancient oaks on the bank had fallen in piles of ash.

Simon Pratt had thought the story was foolishness.

Ruth Oakes had said no one believed it anymore.

Heart had thought it sounded like someone's fancy.

Now, she wasn't so sure.

She glanced at the unicorns. Avamir had lost her horn somehow. Her face was scarred. Moonsilver was beautiful now, but he had been born small and skinny.

He'd had an odd-looking bulge on his forehead when they'd run away from Ash Grove.

Heart had been worried the first time she'd noticed the small, bloody split in Moonsilver's skin—until she realized it was his horn pushing through.

It was growing fast now. The colt rubbed his forehead on trees constantly, trying to ease the itching and stinging.

Heart blinked as the sun edged above the distant mountains.

She missed Ruth Oakes so much.

Ruth had started teaching her about herbs and healing. She had even paid Heart to help her with her work.

"Not that the coins do us any good here," Heart said aloud.

Heart missed Simon in an odd way too.

Her eyes filled with tears.

Simon had not loved her.

But maybe he had never loved anyone.

He had fed her and taught her, and for that she was grateful.

But he was cruel. If he had gotten his way, the unicorns would have been slaughtered for a few pennies.

If Simon had known Avamir and Moonsilver were unicorns, though, he'd have sold them to Tin Blackaby instead.

Heart shivered. If Blackaby learned the truth, he'd send a hundred men into the forest. He'd try to capture the unicorns so he could sell them to Lord Dunraven.

"And if Lord Dunraven ever finds out that you're unicorns, he'll have a thousand men searching," Heart said aloud.

The only way to stay safe was to stay hidden.

She changed camps every night. She kept her cook fires small.

Avamir shook her mane and made a low, whickering sound. Moonsilver cantered to stand close beside his mother.

He was wilder every day, more independent.

He had rubbed off the braided-rag halter and lost it on their first day in the woods. Now, he wouldn't let Heart touch him very often.

Heart's stomach growled and she sighed.

The barley she had brought from Simon's

house was more than half gone. She was trying to make it last.

She saw rabbits and squirrels, but had no way to hunt them.

And winter was coming.

Soon it would snow and the grass would be buried. And they had no shelter from the cold.

Heart kicked at a loose rock and listened to it rattle its way down the slope.

The mare looked up, then went on with her grazing.

"What should I do?" Heart asked the sky.

+ CHAPTER TWO

The chilly nights came and went. Every day, Heart searched for shelter and food.

Then, one misty morning, she saw a shadow at the base of a cliff.

After a long moment, she began to walk up the mountainside.

Avamir lifted her head from grazing as Heart passed.

"Maybe it's a cave," Heart said aloud.

She was getting into the habit of talking to Avamir. She knew it was silly, but it made her feel less lonely.

Avamir whickered at Moonsilver, and they followed as they always did.

Heart waded across a clear little creek.

She slowed, coming up out of the little valley. She was afraid to hope.

Moonsilver galloped in wild circles.

He leaped from one boulder to another.

Heart smiled. No horse colt ever leaped like that. No horse colt ever *could*.

Moonsilver snorted, ducking his head to arch his neck. Avamir leaped sideways, startling him. He bolted into another boulder-jumping circle.

Heart smiled.

Avamir was such a good mother.

"I think it *is* a cave," Heart whispered.

She held her breath, pushing her way through a patch of deer brush. There *was* an opening in the rock!

Avamir slowed, her ears pricked forward.

Caves made good homes for bears, Heart knew. And wolves.

Avamir held her head high. Moonsilver stayed behind her. Heart was ready to run at the slightest sound.

But there was only the silence of the forest.

In front of the opening in the rock, Heart laid one hand on Avamir's withers.

They stood still for a long moment, listening. Then Heart picked up a handful of pebbles and tossed them into the darkness of the cave.

The pebbles hit and rolled to a standstill, then there was silence.

Heart set down her sack.

The silence continued.

She dug through the things she had brought from Simon Pratt's house. Near the bottom of the bag she found the two stubbed candles.

It took several tries to strike a spark into a little pile of dry pine needles.

Once they were burning, Heart lit a candle-wick.

Her pulse thudding, she protected the little flame with one hand. "You stay here," she said to Avamir.

The mare blew out a breath and twitched her tail.

Heart started forward, every muscle in her body tense and ready.

Just inside the cave, she stopped, blinking.

The candlelight flickered in a golden globe around her.

Beyond it, there was midnight darkness.

Heart took one more step. Then another.

The cave was *big*—much bigger than she had dared to hope. She had taken sixteen steps when her candle's light finally struck a wall of gray stone.

Heart lifted the candle, looking straight up.

The rock arched pretty high.

Avamir would be able to walk without lowering her head.

The floor was gritty with sand and pebbles. And it was dry as salt.

Heart allowed herself a hopeful smile.

She would gather firewood every day until they had enough.

She would cut grass and dry it as much as she could before the first snow settled in.

And she would manage, somehow, to build a gate across the entrance to the cave. "We will be safe here," she said aloud.

Her voice sounded hollow and strange.

She felt a sudden wrench of loneliness. But why should she be any lonelier now than she had been in Ash Grove?

Only three people there had ever really talked to her.

Simon had ordered her around. Tibbs Renner, the knacker's son, had found ways to be mean to her. Only Ruth Oakes had been her friend.

Heart turned back toward the entrance.

Avamir and Moonsilver were waiting for her. "It's wonderful," Heart said to Avamir. "Dry and warm and bigger than I thought."

The unicorn mare blew out a long breath and flicked her tail.

Then she came forward lightly.

Moonsilver was right behind her.

+ CHAPTER THREE

Heart walked downhill with the unicorns every morning. Once they had found a meadow with good grass, she set about her own chores.

There was so much to do.

Heart swept a rock shelf in the cave and dried the grass and herbs upon it. She gathered grass and firewood. She found pine nuts and acorns and stored them. She gathered purslane and cress to eat. She built a fire ring of flat stones. She dragged in a wide log to sit upon.

And everywhere Heart walked, she looked for fallen branches.

She searched for long, straight ones.

At night, by firelight, Heart worked on her gate.

Using sharp sticks and a knife she had taken from Simon's house, she dug deep, narrow holes. When each hole was finished, she set a branch upright in it.

But before the gate was finished, she ran out of barley.

"I can eat pine nuts and purslane for a while," she told Avamir one afternoon.

The white mare shook her mane.

She switched her tail sharply.

"I've dried a lot of grass for you," Heart said. She reached out to lay her hand on the mare's neck.

Moonsilver was galloping in wide arcs as usual, playing.

"But I have to go back to Ash Grove to buy food before long," Heart whispered.

She knew Avamir couldn't really understand.

But she needed to say it, anyway.

"I'm afraid to go back," she admitted, "but I want to see Ruth Oakes. She'll worry."

Avamir ticked one forehoof on a pebble, and

it rolled ahead of them. Then she shook her mane and cantered away. Heart watched her gallop, then slow to a trot, then stop in a patch of tall, green grass.

A breeze rising from the valley below rustled the leaves.

Heart looked down the slope, toward the tree-hidden road.

Maybe she should follow it toward Derrytown, not back to Ash Grove.

Derrytown was twenty times the size of Ash Grove, people said. No one would know who she was. No one would notice one more poor girl.

"Look there!"

Heart stumbled to a stop.

It was a man's voice—not close, but not too far away.

Whirling around, Heart scanned the trees.

"Is that a white deer?" a second voice called. "Can you see it?"

Heart followed the shout with her eyes and

spotted a movement in the trees far downhill. A tiny bit of red flashed among the branches, then was gone. A hunter's cap?

"Moonsilver!" Heart whispered frantically, starting to run.

The colt had been cantering joyously.

Heart could tell he had heard the voices.

He was scared, turning sharply to start back toward his mother.

He galloped toward a fallen log, then rose to jump it. His forehooves tucked with a dancer's grace.

Avamir whickered anxiously. Then the air was torn by a terrible shriek.

For an instant, Heart was sure the scream was human.

As she ran, she imagined one of the men doubled over a sprained ankle.

Then she saw Moonsilver pitch to one side, the beautiful arc of his leap ending in a crashing fall.

Avamir lunged into a gallop, her hooves light and nearly soundless on the soft forest soil.

Heart dropped her gathering sack to run faster. "Can you see it?"

The voice was closer, echoing among the trees. The hunters were coming through the thick forest, making their way up the rocky slope.

"No!" came the curt answer. "But I hit it. You heard it cry out."

Heart ran harder, holding her ragged skirts with one hand. If they got close enough to see Moonsilver clearly . . .

As Avamir plunged to a stop beside her colt, Heart veered to run almost straight across the slope. She sprinted, reckless and desperate.

She glanced back twice. Once she was sure that the unicorns were well behind her, she let out a high-pitched wail.

"There it is! Hear it?" came a shout.

"It's heading north," the second voice accused. "You only wounded it!"

The men's voices were still far down the mountainside—so far that Heart realized something as she ran.

To hit Moonsilver from that far, they had to be using crossbows.

Ordinary village men hunted with short bows. Lord Dunraven forbade any other weapon. Only his own men were armed with crossbows.

Heart put every ounce of her will into running.

She ignored the stab of sharp sticks and rocks bruising her bare feet.

She let out another trailing scream as she ran, then fell silent again.

Breathing hard, she heard the men shouting behind her. Good. They were following *her* now.

Heart ran desperately, pounding through the thickest stands of trees to keep the men from seeing her.

She screamed again over her shoulder.

After a long time, Heart veered to the east. She circled, leading the men farther and father from the unicorns.

Finally, she slowed, then stopped, dragging in gasping breaths.

Silent and careful, she found a tall tree to climb.

Breathing hard, she waited, high in the branches.

The afternoon light was fading.

The forest was thick with shadows.

The men passed close enough for her to hear what they were saying.

"I saw it clearly before I shot," one hunter insisted wearily. "It was a snow-white deer."

The other man laughed. "I'll bet it was an old gray pony some Gypsy let loose."

"An old pony wouldn't have made it this far," the first voice argued.

Heart waited until their voices had faded away.

Then she slid down the tree and doubled back.

The sun was setting.

How long had she been away from the unicorns?

Was Moonsilver still alive?

The thought that he might not be struck her with a pain so deep that for a moment, she could not draw in a breath.

✦ CHAPTER FOUR

Heart made her way back through the forest. Fear weighed her feet and chilled her skin.

When she saw Moonsilver standing beside his mother, her spirits leaped upward.

But then she got close enough to see the blood streaming down his hind leg.

The arrow lay half buried in the dirt on the slope above Moonsilver. It had cut a long gash on his right back leg, just above the hock.

Moonsilver's wounded leg would not bear his weight. He stumbled against his mother, then stood trembling.

Heart found her gathering sack where she had dropped it.

She tore the soft cloth into wide strips.

Then she looked intently at Avamir. "Tell him he has to let me do this," she pleaded, wishing the mare really could understand her.

Avamir pawed the ground uneasily.

"I have to bind it," Heart said, trying not to cry, trying not to stare at the blood staining the pine needles.

She talked to Moonsilver in a low, murmuring voice.

Moonsilver looked at Heart. His eyes were distant, glassy. She could tell he was in terrible pain.

She risked a single step forward.

Moonsilver lifted his head sharply, but he didn't move. She took another step.

Avamir reached out to touch Moonsilver's back with her muzzle.

The colt twitched his skin, then held still.

One more step and Heart stood beside him. She reached out very slowly, placing her hand gently on his neck.

Heart paused again, giving Moonsilver time to calm down.

Then she slid her hand along, an inch at a time. The colt stood still.

Heart pressed the cloth against the wound.

Moonsilver had his muzzle almost on the ground. He swayed a little as she wrapped the strips around his leg.

Heart glanced up the mountainside. It was getting darker—and chillier.

Suddenly, Moonsilver fell forward onto his knees.

Heart rushed to put her arms around him, holding him upright. Avamir came close, whickering low.

Heart pulled Moonsilver back up.

He could barely walk.

Still, he managed to start uphill. He had to stop every few steps.

When they finally reached the entrance to their cave, he stumbled inside.

Heart staggered along, helping him, finally letting him sag to the sand near the fire ring.

She built up the fire and warmed creek water to wash the wound.

The bleeding had slowed, but it hadn't stopped.

The wound was deeper than she had thought. Much deeper.

Once it was clean, Heart tightened the bandages a little.

"We need Ruth Oakes," she said to Avamir.

Moonsilver leaned against her.

He laid his head in her lap. Avamir nuzzled him.

"Maybe he'll be stronger in the morning," Heart said aloud.

Of course he would, she thought as she stared into the embers of the fire.

He *had* to be.

Heart lay awake worrying, listening to Moonsilver's breathing. Then sleep overcame her.

But she slept uneasily.

This time it was hunters who chased her across the rocky ground in her dreams.

✦ CHAPTER FIVE

In the morning, Heart woke up suddenly, breathing hard.

Then, her dreams faded away.

Except for her own pounding pulse, the cave was quiet.

Moonsilver was asleep beside her. Avamir was standing over him, her eyes closed and her head low.

Heart got to her feet.

She peeked out the cave entrance, listening.

Morning birds were singing. That meant there were no strangers in the forest.

Heart turned to kneel beside Moonsilver.

She touched him lightly. He did not awaken. His skin felt too warm beneath her hands. Fever?

Heart bit at her lip. He wasn't stronger. He

was weaker. And if the wound went bad—if it swelled and the flesh rotted—he could die. She tried to wake Moonsilver again. He opened his eyes, then closed them again.

A terrible thought came to her.

Every hunter carried one or two poisoned arrows for mountain lions or bears—dangerous animals that weren't easily killed.

Heart stood up, feeling almost dizzy with fear.

She went outside, trying to think.

The treetops below her rolled like a green ocean in the breeze.

Heart caught a distant glimpse of the Derrytown road through the swaying branches.

She took a long breath.

The hunters would come back.

They would search for the mysterious animal they had shot.

Now that it was light out, they'd find her barefoot prints and the unicorn's tracks—and the blood where Moonsilver had stood, trembling.

Heart told herself it would be all right—so long as the hunters didn't see Moonsilver.

The unicorn's hoofprints looked no different from any ordinary horse's. The hunters would think that they had shot a horse colt.

But then what would they do?

Would they keep looking? They might, if they had used poison and thought the animal had to be dead somewhere nearby.

Or maybe they would ride back to Dunraven's castle and never tell anyone, afraid they had killed an old pony by mistake.

Either way, it'd be safe to come back to the cave eventually, Heart thought.

For now, it was a very dangerous place.

Heart ducked back inside.

Avamir was wide awake now, still standing close to Moonsilver.

"Eat all you can," Heart whispered to the mare, piling dried grass beside her.

Heart buried her fire ring with clean, dry sand and hid her cook pot. She hid everything except her flint fire striker and one candle stub—and her coins. She knotted them up in a strip of cloth. Then she took down her unfinished gate.

Last, she used a leafy tree branch to smooth their tracks from the sandy floor.

Walking slowly, with Moonsilver between Heart and Avamir, they left the cave.

The sun was warm and it seemed to strengthen Moonsilver a little.

It was still hard going.

They walked close to the Derrytown road, but stayed out of sight.

Moonsilver would have fallen a dozen times if Heart and his mother hadn't been propping him up from both sides.

Heart's arms ached by noon. By dusk, her legs hurt too, strained from bracing Moonsilver upright.

Heart finally stopped, weary, in a stand of sycamore trees.

They were close.

She could see the shine of the Blue River half a mile ahead.

"We can rest," Heart whispered to Avamir. "We'll wait until dark to cross the bridge."

Heart sighed. Moonsilver was too weak even to consider trying to swim the river. They had to go through the village.

Heart settled Moonsilver on a bed of leaves. He sank to the ground, his eyes closing. Avamir stood over him.

Heart curled up beside Moonsilver, worry numbing the pain of hunger in her stomach.

She lay silently, thinking.

They would have to go straight up Crosswater Street, right through town.

The shops would all be empty and closed, but there were some houses, too.

Suddenly, the clopping of hooves broke the silence of the night.

Heart caught her breath and opened her eyes.

✦ CHAPTER SIX

The moon had risen, full and bright.

Heart lay perfectly still, listening as the hoof-beats got closer.

"Stop following me!"

Heart flinched at the sound of the low, furious voice.

She got to her feet.

Through the trees she saw the shadowy shape of an old flat-bedded farmer's wagon.

The oak wheels were sun bleached, almost shining in the moonlight. The horse drawing it was swaybacked.

Heart glanced at Avamir.

The mare's head was high, her nostrils flared.

Moonsilver was still asleep. His breathing was deep and slow.

"Go back!" the man said over his shoulder.

Heart leaned close to Avamir. "Be still," she breathed. "Be quiet."

Heart heard the creaking of old wood as the wagon passed.

Then she listened hard.

The silence stretched out.

There was no sound of footsteps—nothing. Whoever the man had been arguing with must have followed him.

Heart closed her eyes again and tried to rest.

When she opened them, it was still dark, but Heart sensed it was time to go.

She sat up.

Avamir lowered her head, touching Moonsilver's back with her muzzle. The colt moved a little.

"We have to be careful," Heart whispered.

Moonsilver shivered the skin on his shoulders and back, as though there were summer flies biting him.

Then he opened his eyes.

Avamir nuzzled him again.

Moonsilver lurched up awkwardly, stumbling against his mother.

The stained bandage was tight over his wound.

But Heart could see dark streaks in his white coat. It was still bleeding.

"Wait here," Heart said, reaching out to pat Avamir's scarred forehead gently. "Do you understand? Stay hidden."

The unicorn mare looked into Heart's eyes.

Then Heart turned, making her way through the trees.

She looked both directions down the hard-packed dirt road.

It was empty.

It was hard to get Moonsilver moving again. His leg had stiffened. Avamir and Heart braced him up as well as they could.

Slowly, stopping every few minutes, they made their way eastward.

Heart glanced at the sky.

It wasn't getting light yet, and the moon was still high.

Maybe, with luck, they could make it through the town without being seen.

For a second, Heart imagined Ruth Oakes's warm kitchen, and her eyes flooded with tears.

A short, sharp bark startled her into an abrupt stop. Moonsilver nearly fell, and Heart struggled to steady him.

A patchy-colored puppy was standing stiff-legged in front of them, peering at them in the moonlight. Now Heart understood whom the wagoneer had been scolding.

She looked past the pup, squinting.

The road was empty, and there was no sound of hooves or footsteps.

"Come here," she whispered to the puppy, kneeling down.

The pup tilted its head.

"Come on," Heart said quietly. "I won't hurt you."

The puppy still didn't move.

Heart heard Avamir blow out a soft, fluttery breath.

The puppy whined, a sad, reed-thin sound. Then he lifted his head, and the moonlight lit his face.

One of the puppy's eyes was deep brown.

The other was light blue.

Heart knelt and reached out to the puppy. He bolted into her arms. He was shaking, whimpering. He was almost too big to hold.

Avamir let out a longer, noisier breath.

Heart looked at her. "I know."

Avamir stamped a forehoof.

Heart stood up, gently sliding the pup back to the ground.

He let out another sharp bark.

"Kip?" Heart said, making the sound into a word. "I'm sorry, but you can't come with us, Kip."

Heart knew she had no choice.

If the pup barked going through town, he'd start every dog in Ash Grove howling. *Someone* would come look.

Moonsilver had lowered his head, his muzzle nearly touching the ground again.

Heart moved away slowly, making sure the colt was leaning against Avamir.

She clapped her hands suddenly, startling the puppy into leaping backward. "Shoo!"

The pup scrambled to get away from her.

Heart's eyes filled with tears.

She hated scaring him.

But what else could she do? It was too dangerous to let him follow them through Ash Grove. If she could have carried him—but she couldn't.

"Go on!" she said, clapping once more. "Go!" The puppy ran this time, disappearing into the darkness of the trees.

Heart took her place by Moonsilver, and they began to walk.

She glanced back.

The pup wasn't coming.

Her eyes stung and overflowed. She freed one hand long enough to swipe at the tears.

Then she went on.

+ CHAPTER SEVEN

The sound of the unicorns' hooves on the bridge planks made Heart uneasy.

The night around them seemed too quiet.

At least there were no houses at this end of Crosswater Street.

As they came off the bridge onto the cobblestones, Heart pushed gently at Avamir's neck, guiding her to the side of the street.

In the gutter, mud and leaves muffled their hoofbeats.

They passed Market Square.

Heart barely breathed as they went.

There was no stirring of wind, no rain or distant thunder—nothing to cover the sound of their passing.

Moonsilver was unsteady.

They passed the last of the shops across from Market Square.

Avamir walked slower and slower—because Moonsilver did.

"Please, just keep going," Heart whispered to him as they passed the first of the houses.

The windows were all dark.

The second and third houses were dark as well.

So was the fourth.

The fifth and sixth houses were silent and lifeless.

But inside the seventh, a dog began to bark.

Heart tried to go a little faster.

It was impossible.

Moonsilver was tottering, barely able to walk.

The barking got louder.

The colt suddenly staggered and fell forward, crashing onto his knees. Heart stood over him, trying to drag him upright. He did his best, his hooves skidding on the cobblestones.

The dog kept barking, a quick, jarring rhythm.

Heart glanced at the house.

The front door opened.

The flicker of a candle-lantern shone dimly.

"Is someone there?" a voice from inside the house asked.

"I can't see anything." The answer came from the doorway.

A sudden sharp bark near Heart's feet made her spin around.

"Hush," she hissed at the pup. "Hush!" But the puppy yapped again.

"It's just some stray dog," the doorway-voice announced.

There were footsteps.

Then the amber glow of the candle-lantern disappeared. Heart heard the door close.

Kip stopped barking and stood close to her leg.

Heart touched his head gently.

Then she tried once more to help Moonsilver up.

This time, he made it.

Shaking with effort and fear, Heart steadied the colt as they went on.

She glanced back.

The puppy was trotting off to one side, stopping to sniff at the cobblestones.

His patchy colors made him look like a small cluster of moving shadows in the fading moonlight.

When Heart looked again, he was gone.

Tirin Bridge arched over its creek. On the far side, the cobblestones were older, rougher. Heart tried not to scrape her bare toes.

They made the turn at the end of Crosswater Street.

Heading south on the River Road was easier. The soft dust gave them firmer footing, and Moonsilver could go a little faster.

Heart looked up.

The moon was setting, and the sun would rise soon.

It didn't matter now.

They were getting close to Crooked Lane.

When Heart saw a lantern shining in Ruth Oakes's window, she felt tears rise in her eyes again.

Ruth was up very early, as usual.

The unicorns stood quietly on the garden walk, Moonsilver leaning on Avamir.

Heart inhaled the strong scent of rosemary and hyssop.

Then she stepped up to the door and knocked.

Ruth Oakes opened her door and looked out. Her eyes went wide. "I was so worried, child," she said, opening her arms to hug Heart.

✦ CHAPTER EIGHT

"A hunter shot the colt . . . ," Heart began. The breathless story came rushing out.

Ruth listened, then raised one hand. "Let's put the mare in the old pasture and—"

"No," Heart interrupted. "No one can see them."

"Dunraven's men have long gone," Ruth said calmly. "There's no reason to—"

But before she could finish, Heart stood aside. The lantern light spilled out the door onto Moonsilver and Avamir.

Moonsilver's horn gleamed in the amber glow.

Ruth pulled in a sudden breath. "Oh, my." She covered her mouth with one hand. "Then the mare's scar . . . ? Oh, my!"

Heart stood still, waiting.

Ruth Oakes motioned. "Let's bring them both inside, then."

Heart nodded, grateful for Ruth Oakes's calmness, for her steadiness.

In half an hour, the healer had them all settled.

A storage room became an open stall for Avamir.

The mare stood looking at her colt as Heart told Ruth Oakes everything that had happened.

Moonsilver was lying in front of the hearth as they talked.

Ruth had put herbs and a clean bandage on his wound. He was sound asleep.

It was such a heavy, deep sleep that it scared Heart.

"Will he be all right?"

Ruth arched her brows. "Why don't you wash your face and sleep a few hours before you start to worry about—"

"Will he?" Heart interrupted.

Ruth sighed. "I don't know."

Heart felt her stomach tighten. "Is it poison?"

Ruth shrugged. "I used the spikenard in case."

"The hunter thought Moonsilver was a white deer. I heard him say it," Heart told her.

Ruth Oakes nodded. "Then he wouldn't care if the meat was spoiled. He just wanted to prove what he'd seen."

Heart winced. "I had the same thought."

Ruth nodded. She put another log on the fire. Then she wiped her hands on her apron.

When she spoke again, her voice was soft. "The legends say unicorns can heal with their horns and—"

Avamir stamped a forehoof, and Ruth turned to face her.

Heart turned too.

Avamir had no horn now, only the wide, leathery scar.

Heart looked at Moonsilver again.

The colt lay so still.

His ribs rose and fell a little with his breathing.

Heart glanced at Avamir. The mare's eyes seemed full of sadness.

Ruth seemed to have the same thought. "It's hurting her not to be able to help."

"I love them," Heart said, without meaning to.

Ruth Oakes smiled. "Clearly. And they love you." She straightened her apron. "Unicorns!" her voice was full of wonder. "I always hoped the stories were true."

A sharp bark outside the door made Heart look up.

"Is this someone else you know?" Ruth asked, smiling.

Heart nodded slowly, explaining about the puppy.

Ruth rose and went to the door.

The puppy came in slowly, his head low, his tail tucked.

Then he saw Heart and bounded into her arms.

In the lantern light she could see his eyes more

clearly. The blue one was summer-sky blue.

"I thought Kip stopped following us," Heart told Ruth. She told her how the puppy had saved them by barking.

Ruth nodded. "Kip?"

The puppy looked up.

Ruth met Heart's eyes. "If you've named him, he's yours."

Heart shook her head. "I can't take care of him. I can't take care of anyone." She covered her mouth with one hand, fighting tears.

"You already have," Ruth said firmly.

Without another word she brought blankets and made a pallet beside Moonsilver.

Heart managed to wash her face and hands.

Then she lay down. Kip curled up against her back.

Heart closed her eyes, and sleep came almost instantly. For once, she didn't dream.

She woke by noon.

That first day was terrible.

Moonsilver barely stirred.

When he did, his eyes were clouded. He would not eat.

Kip whined and circled the room. Avamir stood uneasily in the storeroom doorway, staring at her colt.

Ruth cleaned the wound twice, sealing it with meadowsweet salve after each washing.

She steeped a pot of feverfew tea.

Then she added a dark powder Heart had never seen before.

"Cohosh and spikenard, in equal parts," Ruth said when she noticed Heart was watching.

Moonsilver drank a little of the mixture, then closed his eyes and sank back into sleep.

Heart watched, wishing she could stay forever in this sunny house.

The day went by very slowly.

Moonsilver slept most of the time.

When he woke for a few minutes, in the afternoon, he would not eat. He drank a little more of the tea.

Heart sat beside him.

Avamir stood close, all day, watching her colt.

Ruth Oakes gave Kip a bone to chew. He gnawed it and carried it around. Then he settled into a nap.

On the third morning, Heart woke early.

Ruth was sleeping—so were the unicorns.

Heart slipped outside. Kip wanted to follow, but she shut him in.

In the cover of the morning fog, she ran down to the river to cut grass. Going each way, she passed just within sight of Simon's house. It looked smaller and sadder than ever.

In the evening, once it was almost dark, Heart took Avamir out for a gallop.

Waiting for the mare to canter back to her, Heart was swept with sadness.

Everything felt so familiar.

It felt safe—even though she knew it wasn't.

She wanted to learn about herbs and healing from Ruth Oakes like she had before.

She wanted to stay in Ash Grove.

And she knew she couldn't.

On the fourth morning, Moonsilver untangled his long legs and stood up.

Heart ran outside to bring in a bundle of grass she'd cut by the river.

The colt ate eagerly.

Ruth Oakes smiled. "He's past it now."

Heart looked at her. "Was it poison?"

Ruth nodded. "The hunter chose an arrow to make sure he died, good shot or bad."

"I want to stay here," Heart said quietly.

"You could," Ruth Oakes said. "But they cannot." She gestured at Avamir and Moonsilver.

Heart nodded. "So as soon as Moonsilver is strong, we'll leave."

"Back to the cave you told me about?" Ruth Oakes asked.

Heart shrugged. "We'll be safe there."

Ruth Oakes leaned toward her and touched her cheek. "I will bring you whatever you need. We'll meet on the road."

Heart found herself grinning. "You would do that?"

Ruth laughed. "That and more."

"You will have to be very careful," Heart said quietly.

Ruth nodded. "Indeed, we both will." She stretched. "I'll be gone when you get up tomorrow. I'll be home around noontime."

"Is someone sick?" Heart asked.

Ruth nodded. "A sweet old woman. I should have gone yesterday."

Heart nodded.

"I want to give you something, before you go," Ruth said. She reached into her apron pocket and took out a tiny silk pouch. "My grandmother gave me this."

Heart opened the pouch. Inside was a silvery thread, coiled into a circle.

"My grandmother gave it to me when I was your age. She said it was magic, that it would protect me."

Heart touched the shining thread. It felt warm.

Ruth smiled. "Now it can protect you."

"Thank you," Heart said, then hugged Ruth Oakes.

The old woman smiled again. "Now sleep, child."

Heart nodded. She was tired. She straightened out her blankets and settled in for the night.

In her dreams she was running, as always, but she wasn't as afraid this time. She ran faster—so fast that the rocky ground blurred beneath her feet.

✦ CHAPTER NINE

The next morning, Heart woke early, as always.

Ruth had already left.

The house felt empty without her in it. Heart got up and dressed, careful to be quiet.

Avamir was awake.

Moonsilver slept, but it was a normal sleep, a healing sleep now.

Kip sat up, watching her. When she went out, he slipped past her and scrambled through the door before she could close it.

Heart tried to catch him to put him back inside. He ran in circles, dodging her easily.

"I'm not playing, Kip," Heart whispered. "You have to go inside!"

Kip ignored her.

He leaped aside when she reached to grab him.

Heart clenched her fists. "I have to go get grass!" she scolded.

Kip reversed direction and ran close enough for her to lunge at him—and miss.

Heart frowned.

There was no real reason the pup couldn't come with her.

The fog was as thick as cotton.

They would be well hidden.

Almost no one ever came this far south of town—especially not this early in the morning.

There was nothing but sagebrush past Simon's house—sagebrush and the Blue River.

Heart started off.

Kip stayed close to her heels.

She followed Crooked Lane until she could see Simon's place through the fog.

Then she veered off through the sage.

Kip ran ahead, then came back.

The Blue River was beautiful, Heart thought as she walked down the long slope.

As always, she glanced toward the place Simon had found her, lying asleep in the grass.

As always, she tried to recall something from before that day.

Maybe I never will, she told herself.

The thought didn't upset her as much as usual.

She wasn't sure why, but she was grateful.

Heart set about her work.

The fog made her shiver, but she was glad it was so thick this morning. Kip splashed in the shallows. He chased a rabbit, then came back.

"Come, Kip," Heart called once she had the grass bundled.

The pup stopped playing and ran toward her.

They started back.

Heart stayed well away from Simon's house, angling northward toward Crooked Lane.

When she stepped out of the sagebrush onto the road, she sighed in relief. Her feet were sore from walking.

"Girl? Is that you?" Simon's rasping voice startled Heart so badly that she dropped the bundle of grass.

"Where have you been?"

Heart opened her mouth to say something, but no words came out.

"Where are the horses?" he demanded. "Did you put them back into the old pen?"

"They aren't here," Heart said.

Simon spat into the sagebrush. "Did you sell them?"

His face was even sharper than Heart had remembered.

She saw him step forward, but she could not move.

She saw him reaching out to grab her arm.

She still could not move.

Kip barked suddenly. Simon jerked backward as the pup jumped between them. Kip stood stiff-legged and solid, growling at him.

"And a pup now, too?" Simon demanded. "You can't come home with a pup."

"I'm not," Heart said, cutting him off.

Simon looked like she had slapped him. "What?"

"I'm not coming back," Heart said. She scooped up the grass. "Avamir and Moonsilver are mine. I have taken care of her and fed her and I've taken care of the colt. And I left you money for everything else."

"You are ungrateful—" Simon began, but she interrupted him.

"I am not. But I am never coming back."

Heart strode away, Kip following at her heels.

Back at Ruth Oakes's house, she laid down the grass. Moonsilver ate eagerly. Avamir crossed the room to join him.

Simon would be angry, Heart knew. He would be watching.

Heart clenched her fists. She wanted so much to stay. But she couldn't. Not now.

Heart went into the kitchen.

She filled the gathering sack with leftover bread and some dry barley. She took a few carrots, and some herbs, too.

Then she unknotted the strip of cloth that held her coins.

She left half her money beside the kitchen basin.

Ruth would never ask her to pay, Heart knew. But she felt good doing it, anyway.

Heart took a length of flax rope from Ruth's storeroom.

She knotted it into a halter.

From a distance, at least, Avamir would have to look like an ordinary horse.

"We have to go now," she told the unicorns.

They were busy with the grass. "We have to go now," Heart repeated urgently, touching Avamir's neck. The unicorn mare allowed Heart to slide the halter on.

She lifted her head and looked into Heart's eyes. Then she turned and nuzzled Moonsilver.

Together they left Ruth Oakes's house.

Kip stayed close to Heart's heels.

Moonsilver limped, but he walked with his head high. Heart closed the door softly, silently, wondering if she would ever see Ruth again.

✦ CHAPTER TEN

Heart was afraid to go through town—but she was more afraid to try to swim the unicorns across the Blue River.

"Stay close, Kip," she said as they turned off the River Road and started down Crosswater Street.

The fog was thick.

It was as if the town had disappeared.

Heart could hear a cow mooing in someone's pens, ready to be milked.

The sound seemed muffled and far away.

Even the clopping of the unicorn's hooves on the cobblestones seemed softer in the fog.

Wagon wheels grinding on the stones warned Heart in time to push Moonsilver behind his mother. Then she walked close to Avamir's head, holding the rope, as though she was leading the mare.

The cart driver barely glanced at them.

Heart swallowed hard.

There were going to be more wagons. But what choice did she have? She had to leave before Simon managed to see Moonsilver's horn.

Avamir stayed close as they walked—just the right distance for a horse being led along. Moonsilver stayed behind her. Kip barked at vague shapes in the fog, but he was quiet when a wagon passed.

"Good, Kip," Heart praised him, glad that the pup knew better than to startle cart horses.

They were almost past Market Square and heading for the Blue River Bridge when Heart saw two familiar shapes in the fog ahead.

Tibbs Renner and his mother were on their way to market.

No one walked with them.

Heart knew why. They always smelled of the knacker's yard.

Mrs. Renner turned toward Market Square without seeing Heart, but Tibbs stared.

Heart felt her stomach tighten. She glanced over her shoulder. Moonsilver was staying close to Avamir's flank. Tibbs couldn't have seen him.

As Heart watched, he walked on with his mother.

He'd wait for a chance to say something mean to her at market, she was sure.

"But I won't be here," Heart whispered, watching the fog swallow him and his mother.

Heart gripped the rope and walked faster.

Her feet were cold and sore.

The cobblestones grated at her skin.

When they finally reached the Blue River Bridge, Heart pulled in a long breath.

They were going to make it.

And they were in luck.

The bridge was empty. If they hurried, they wouldn't have to pass too close to a wagon headed to market.

The fog had wet the planks as though it had rained.

Heart slipped once and steadied herself against Avamir.

Kip stayed close, trotting carefully.

Heart saw him looking downward through the cracks between the planks at the water below.

Stepping off the bridge, Heart listened.

There was no sound of hooves or wagon wheels.

"Halt!"

The man's voice seemed to come out of nowhere.

Heart spun around, trying to spot him.

"Stop where you are," the voice ordered.

Then the man stepped close enough for Heart to see him. She didn't know his face, but she knew who he was. Or what he was, anyway. He wore the gray shirt that all of Tin Blackaby's hired men wore.

"Where'd you get these horses?"

Heart glanced back at Avamir. She had

positioned herself between the man and Moonsilver. He could not see the colt.

"I found the mare in the forest," she said, telling the truth.

"We have someone here who says different," the man said.

It was only then that Heart saw Simon standing off to one side. The old man was sweating, breathing hard. He must have run all the way from his house, straight across the fields to Tin Blackaby's house.

Heart glanced around.

"The horses are mine, of course," Simon was saying. "I bought the mare from a Gypsy. I took this child in. Everyone knows that."

Tin Blackaby's man nodded.

"You are free to go, if you like," he said. "But the horses are Simon's property. He complained of the theft weeks ago."

The man stepped closer.

He reached out so quickly that Heart could not react. He caught her arm.

Heart stared at Simon.

He looked angry.

At what? She had been grateful to him for taking care of her, for teaching her how to cook, how to gather barley. She had worked so hard in his house.

"I'll buy the horses from you, Simon," she said aloud.

She stepped toward him, then glanced back.

Moonsilver was still hidden behind Avamir. Only his legs and hooves showed.

Tin Blackaby's man laughed again. "Buy? With what?"

Heart pulled her arm free and reached into her carry sack. She untied the cloth and took out some coins.

"Where'd you steal that?" the man asked.

Heart looked at Simon.

He knew very well she had worked for the coins.

He had taken a share of the money Ruth had paid her. She pressed her lips together.

She didn't want to give Tin Blackaby's man any reason to watch Ruth Oakes.

The sound of boot heels on the bridge behind her made Heart look up.

She saw two more of Tin Blackaby's men coming through the mist.

In seconds, they would be able to see Moonsilver.

"We've caught old Simon's horse thief," the man beside Heart called to them.

"Goat thief, too," the other man shouted back. "Hey, what *is* that? A colt?"

Heart whirled around and pulled the halter off Avamir so the rope wouldn't tangle and trip her. "Run! Get away!"

Heart jumped aside as the unicorn mare reared, lunging into a gallop.

Tin Blackaby's man was knocked sideways.

Moonsilver leaped over him to follow his mother.

In an instant, they were gone, their white coats blending with the fog.

"Get that girl!" the fallen man shouted.

Kip barked sharply as Heart began to run.

She heard him snarling, and glanced back.

Kip was darting in and out of the men's legs, snapping and growling. One of them stumbled, cursing.

Kip sprang away and raced after her.

Heart headed for the trees, clutching her bag as she ran.

"Hurry!" a man's voice came through the fog. "She won't get far!"

Heart veered away, guided by the men's voices as they shouted to one another.

Her bare feet were silent in the dust.

Their boots thudded heavily.

She changed direction again when she reached the edge of the forest.

Heart heard Simon's voice, muffled in the fog, shouting her name.

She slowed enough to look back.

She could hear Simon and Tin Blackaby's men, but she couldn't see them through the fog.

That meant they couldn't see her.

Heart dodged around a huge oak tree, then ran on, heading into the deep woods.

Kip appeared out of the fog. He ran beside her.

Heart angled her direction again. Slowly, the shouts behind them faded.

Heart ran until her legs ached. She ran until her breath was painful.

Then, finally, she stopped—and listened.

She held perfectly still.

Kip stood leaning against her leg, panting.

Heart picked him up and held him close. "Be quiet," she whispered to him.

Kip wriggled in her arms, but he didn't bark. And all around them, there was only silence.

After a long time, Heart began making her way through the woods, staying well back from the road.

It was almost dark when she got back to the cave.

She walked slowly, coming up the slope carefully, listening.

It was silent.

There were no voices, no hoofbeats, nothing beyond the normal stirrings of mice in the pine needles.

Heart bit at her lower lip. If the unicorns weren't here . . . if they were lost, or hurt . . . Her eyes flooded with tears.

She wiped them away and started upward, Kip at her heels.

The pup yipped once as they topped the rise.

He bounded ahead of her, then ran straight into the cave.

Heart listened to be sure nothing had moved into the cave during her absence. Then she followed Kip inside.

If the unicorns weren't here tonight, she told herself, they would be in the morning.

"If nothing happened," Heart whispered, and her eyes filled with tears again.

Kip barked sharply.

"Hush!" Heart scolded, setting down her sack.

She felt her way along the cave wall for the place where she had hidden her supplies.

Fumbling through the little pile, she finally found a candle stub.

Then she patted the sandy floor until she had found a few wisps of dried grass.

She twisted them together.

The spark from her striker caught the grass on fire.

As the little flame came to life, Heart stood up straight.

Kip yipped again.

Heart turned to shush him.

Then she caught her breath and stared.

Avamir was standing near the back wall of the cave. Beside her, Moonsilver lay sleeping peacefully.

Heart ran to hug the mare's neck.

Avamir lowered her head, and Heart felt her warm breath on her cheek.

Heart felt an odd lightness inside herself. It took her a long moment to realize what it was.

She didn't know where she would get more food now that she couldn't go back to Ash Grove. Blackaby's men would be searching the woods, and she didn't want to endanger Ruth.

She wasn't sure where they could go or what they could do.

She knew only one thing.

For the first time in her life, she wasn't lonely.

Just before Heart fell asleep, she put her hand into her pocket.

She touched the little silk pouch that held Ruth Oakes's silvery thread.

Maybe it *could* protect her. Maybe it already had.